I'll

Remember

McKayla Jacobs

This book is dedicated to me

I did this for me, not for anyone else

hugs

~1~

I took a deep breath, I felt the wind on my shoulders, I could feel the blood dripping from my wrists into the palm of my hand. I looked down at the water below me, it looked almost peaceful, it looked like a better ending.

The bridge shook as the cars drove on it, with every shake I felt closer to the edge. The air was cold, it was winter but it was turning into spring. It was winter and I was in a tank top and shorts.

I just walked from my house and decided that I couldn't take it anymore. My tank top was stained with blood, I stood in a puddle of my own blood, the red stained my feet .

I could feel someone approaching me. His

footsteps seemed familiar and a police officer

walked towards me. He asked,

"What happened?" I knew his voice, how

could I forget it? I answered,

"He's drinking again, he came into my room

and he just started punching and kicking. I couldn't

take it, not this time." He asked,

"What happened to your wrists?" I looked

down, I couldn't look him in the eyes. I asked,

"What's it look like?" He answered,

"Caitlyn, can I take you home?" I

swallowed, my throat burned as I inhaled the cold

air, I answered,

"I'm not going back there, I can't go back

not again." He nodded and asked,

"What can I do?" I answered,

"Can you make sure he gets help? Can you make sure he doesn't hurt anyone else? Can you make sure Ian knows?" I closed my eyes and I could feel myself let go. I just let my mind slip but my feet stayed on the ground. I could feel him grab my wrist. He said,

"I can't let you jump." He pulls me off the bridge holding my wrists as they throb, he puts me in a cop car and takes me to the hospital. As I sat in the cop car I kept my head out the window, I admired the beauty of the outside. My mind gets lost in the trees, as I stare out the window I could hear him talking to me but it was too quiet to make out. It was like the static behind the radio, I could only hear my thoughts, like the music and the static was him talking. I asked,

4

"Where are you taking me?" He kept his eyes on the road as he answered,

"To the hospital, your father will meet us there." I rolled my eyes and mumbled,

"Your brother is a coward! He has to beat his own daughter to feel good about himself! I'm not going back there!" He asked,

"What if I get him help?" I rolled my eyes and answered,

"We've tried this already! He won't get better! He won't let himself get better!" I added, "I can't keep being a human punching bag, I'm not telling you this as a cop. I'm telling you this as my uncle. Please don't make me go back!" He shook his head and said,

"You have to go back, he's your father." I sit back in my seat and close my eyes. My uncle was never the one to disagree, he was always about being quiet about your personal life and putting on a smile when you're out in public. He craved a perfect family, he needed the perfect family image. Yet life isn't about the perfect image, it's a rough image and he knows that better than anyone.

The hospital bandaged up my wrists, nothing major. They must see hundreds of teens and think it's for attention and don't even bother looking again. My father showed up at the hospital, I knew that he was still drunk, he was stumbling and slurring his words.

It doesn't take a genius to figure out when he's drunk, he tends to be violent. He walks into the room, my uncle standing at the foot of the bed like the coward he was, he can't even stand up to his own brother. My uncle exclaimed,

"You told me you were sober!" For the first time he yelled,

"I was! I was until she pushed me!" He pointed at me, it was always my fault, he found a way to blame me for everything. He blamed me for my mother leaving, He blamed me for everything snf sad part was that I believed him. He mumbled, "she's the reason she left!" I yelled,

"She left because she couldn't put up with your abuse! She left because of you and I don't blame her anymore!" My uncle was staring at me as the words slipped out, I wasn't the quiet little girl he knew anymore.

My father walked towards me and grabbed my face, squeezing my cheeks. He tried to intimidate me, and most of the time he did, He whispered,

"It was your fault! You were such a disappointment, she was so embarrassed that's why she left!" I shook my head, I knew that he was lying, I wanted to believe he was lying but maybe he was right. Maybe I was a disappointment, why else would he need to drink?

My uncle and father stepped outside, I took a deep breath as my eyes filled. I covered my mouth as I sobbed.

I could hear his yelling from outside of the door. I called my brother, he was away at college and I just needed someone to talk to. The phone rang three times before he picked up. I took a deep breath and he answered,

"Hello?" I answered,

"Hey, how's college?" Ian asked,

"What's going on?" He could hear the shakiness in my voice. I answered,

"Dad's drinking again." He asked,

"Didn't you tell me he was sober?" I answered,

"He was, for a week, but by day three he started to get angry again." He asked,

"Did he touch you?" I closed my eyes, he knew the answer. I answered,

"Nothing that hasn't happened before." I could hear shuffling through the phone. He said,

"I'm gonna kill him." I said,

"I only have two more years, I can handle the two more years. I need you to focus on school, I need you to be successful and prove to him that we don't need him." He asked,

"Is this a goodbye speech?" I answered,

"I don't know what's gonna happen tonight. He's mad, the most mad I've ever seen him." The line disconnected, I don't know why but I had a bad feeling. My uncle came back in the room and said,

"Your father signed your discharge papers."

I asked,

"After all I told you, you're just gonna let him go? Just let me go with him and face the consequences, you coward!" He walked out of the room, he didn't believe me. No one ever did, and no one will.

My father came in the room and stood in the doorway, he reeked of alcohol. Which didn't surprise me, for as long as I could remember he was a drunk. He would be 'sober' for about a week but then he'd get so angry because the alcohol made him feel better, it made his life better. He watched me as I got up from the bed, his back up against the door frame. He asked,

"How could you be so stupid?" I clenched my jaw and walked past him. As we walked out into the parking lot he grabbed me by my hair pulling me down to the ground. I didn't make a sound, eventually you get used to the pain. He yelled, "if you ever tell anyone again I swear to god you will regret it! Do you understand?" I answered,

"Yes sir." As I got up he walked in front of me. Not looking back, not caring. When I walk in the house it smells like an ashtray, nothing new.

I walked straight to my room, if you keep your head down and he's drunk enough you won't be a punching bag. He came in my room, he sat on the edge of my bed and asked,

"Why do you make me do this?" I answered,

"I don't make you do it! You get drunk and all your feelings come up, and I guess someone has to pay the consequences." He forms a fist and his fist meets my eye, wasn't the first time and definitely won't be the last. I could hear him mumble, "you should've jumped." I should've, and I wished I did.

~2~

I woke up, put on some ripped jeans, a white t-shirt, and put makeup over my eye, it would only be worse if anyone saw it. He was asleep on the couch when I left, I knew he wouldn't be there when I got home. He was always gone when I got home but by midnight he was home.

I care for him, I do and that probably won't ever change. He's my father, he will always be my father. He won't ever be my dad, he'll always be a father.

A dad is someone who cares for his child, who cares for their well being. A father is someone who helped create you.

I get on the bus, it's quiet. It's always quiet in the morning but today, something's different. It's an eerie silence, maybe I was just paranoid but it felt different.

When I got off the bus I could feel the cold breeze on my face. It felt like needles being stuck inside of my face. I felt someone come up behind me, tugging on my arm. The voice behind me said,

"Hey." I look back and roll my eyes, I asked,

"What do you want?" he answered,

"Oh come on, am I that much of a terrible person?" I asked,

"Do you want me to answer that?" He rolled his eyes and answered,

"No." Maverick Parker, the guy who thinks every girl wants him. I said,

"Not today, you can go back to hating me tomorrow." He asked,

"You think I hate you?" I asked,

"Isn't it obvious?" He stood in front of me, stopping me. He answered,

"I don't hate you." I laughed and said,

"Whatever." He grabbed my arm and said,

"I don't hate you!" I yelled,

"Okay! Why is it so important that I know you don't hate me?" He answered,

"Because it just is!" I pull my arm away from him and walk into the building. He stood in his tracks as I walked towards the door. As I walked the halls I could feel eyes on me,

I could feel eyes burning the back on my neck. I opened my locker and the girl beside me giggled as I stood at my locker. I slammed my locker and asked,

"What's so funny? What could possibly be so funny?" They stopped laughing, one of the girls looked at me and pointed to my eye. She whispered,

"You missed a spot." I touched my eye and reopened my locker, I looked in the little mirror hanging on the locker door. The corner of my eye was black, I rolled my eyes and slammed my locker. I snuck out of the doors, the side doors where there were no cameras. I saw him,

I was dreading walking past him. As I

walked out of the parking lot, with my head down

basically holding my breath, hoping he wouldn't see

me. He called,

"As I live and breathe, the girl who never

skips." I sigh, he kept walking towards me. He

grabbed my arm, I pulled my arm away and yelled,

"Don't touch me!" He backed away with his

hands up, he smiled and said,

"Sorry princess." I yelled,

"Don't call me that!" He asked,

"Alright, so what should I call you?" I

answered,

"Oh I don't know, how about my name?"

He smiled and asked,

"That wouldn't be fun would it?" I stopped

in my tracks and turned around. I said,

"Life's not meant to be fun." He asked,

"Then what's the point?" I answered,

"Let me know when you find out." He
asked,

"Where you going?" I answered,

"Home." He said,

"Come with me, we can go to the beach. It's
a decent day." I asked,

"Are you insane? My father would kill me."
He asked,

"Isn't he gonna know anyway? You're
probably gonna get grounded anyway, let's make it
worth it." Make it worth it? If he only knew half of
it. I answered,

"I don't think so, it's not a good idea." He
said,

"Come on, live a little! I'll have you home by the end of the school day." I rolled my eyes, on one hand it could be fun but did I really want to risk it? Did I want to risk fighting with him? Fighting with my father always ended badly, why would this time be different? I asked,

"Where are we going?" He smiled and answered,

"To the beach." I asked,

"In the middle of winter?" He answered,

"It's almost spring, it'll warm up once we get there." He waved his finger in the air as we walked to his car. He opened the car door and I hopped into the passenger side seat. He got in the car after he closed my door, his car was small but nice.

He tapped his fingers on the steering wheel as we drove. He asked, "can you swim?" I answered,

"Never taught." He looks at me and asked,

"Really?" I answered,

"My father isn't one for being around people." He nodded and asked,

"Have you ever been to a beach?" I answered,

"Nope." He asked,

"So what you're telling me is that I'm taking you to the beach for the first time?" I answered,

"Alright calm down, we don't want your ego to get any bigger." He laughed and said,

"I am so honored." I rolled my eyes and stared out the window, watched as we passed the trees, there became less trees as we got closer. The weather started to get warmer but not warm enough

for my foot to even touch the water. He announced,

"So change of plans, we're going to a lake

because cops showed up at the beach, they'll bust us

if we go. A bunch of us skipped today so we're just

gonna go to the lake and have a couple beers." I

asked,

"How many is a bunch?" He answered,

"Like 10 guys, but I promise they won't

give you a hard time." I rolled my eyes and

mumbled,

"Why did I think this would be a good

idea?" He smiled and asked,

"You do that a lot?" I asked,

"Do what?" He smiled and answered,

"Talk to yourself." I smiled and answered,

"Yeah, I like to fill the silence." He smiles and said,

"It's cute." I smile and look out the window again, I could feel his eyes on me. We took back roads, a lot of trees, and a lot of peace. It seemed more peaceful out here, more safe. It felt like a different time, a different world almost. It felt like nothing wrong could happen here because it was peaceful and seemed gentle.

Just like life, it may seem a certain way, it may be perceived a certain way but in the end it's the experiences that make the memories and how one feels in a certain place.

~3~

We parked on the side of the road, he opened the car door and said,

21

"You don't have to swim or anything, just relax and hang out." I nodded, he saw one of his friends and ran off. I sat on the ground, just watching. There were only two other girls there, they came and sat beside me. I kept to myself a lot, I never really talked to anyone because it always ends badly. One of the girls announced,

"I'm Lainey, this is Eliza." I smiled and said,

"Caitlyn." Lainey asked,

"Is Maverick your boyfriend?" I laughed, when I realized it wasn't a joke I answered,

"No, I'm not his girlfriend." She looks at him, I look in his direction and he stares at us. She said,

"I think you better tell him that." I smile when he looks away. She smiled and added, "maybe

you should tell yourself that too." She smiles, I
smile and said,

"We're just friends." She asked,

"Are you telling me or yourself?" I smiled, I
think I was telling myself. She got up but Eliza
stayed. Eliza whispered,

"You're the only girl he's ever brought here.
Interesting isn't it?" I watch him jump of the rock
and into the water as I said,

"Maybe." She smiled and got up, I sat there.
I was admiring the water, how it always moved and
how it kept going for miles. How no matter how
much it rained it always moved forward, how it
never stood still. I could feel someone's wet hands
on my back. I said,

"You're soaked!" He smiled and sat next to
me, then laid his head on my lap. He looked up at

me and smiled, I looked down at him, his eyes were drawing me in. I smiled and asked, "what?" He answered,

"You're beautiful." I smiled and laughed, he moved the hair away from my face. In that moment it felt like the world stopped, I would remember this very moment. I'll remember how he made me feel at that moment. I cupped my face and sat up, he kissed me. In that moment I felt like I was doing the right thing, but in the back of mind my father was there reminding me of how worthless I was.

I pulled away but a smile came across my face. It didn't matter what my father was saying in the back of my mind, I deserved to be happy. I deserve to be able to be appreciated. I smiled and asked,

"Is this why you wanted me to come today?"

He answered,

"Maybe." I smiled and said,

"Interesting." He smiled and laid back down

on my lap. I asked, "shouldn't you be with your

friends?" He answered,

"I'd rather be here with you." I said,

"I'll be here when you get back." He shook

his head, I smiled and said, "go, they're waiting for

you." He gets up and sticks his hand out. He said,

"Then come with me." I take his hand and

we go sit with them, they're laughing and drinking.

Maverick asked, "you wanna drink?" I answered,

"No, I don't drink." He nodded and said,

"Okay." One of his friends whispered,

"Boring." Maverick said,

"She doesn't have to drink if she doesn't

want to! That's her choice!" His friend but his

hands up and said,

"My bad dude, don't shoot. Calm down!"

He was laughing, but it wasn't funny. Maverick

shook his head and whispered,

"Cait, I'm sorry." I said,

"It's okay." He nodded, I didn't drink

because I didn't like the effects. I didn't like how it

made me feel, I didn't like how people acted when

they were drunk.

Maverick went back in the water, I stayed

sitting, Lainey came back to where I was sitting and

sat next to me. She asked,

"It doesn't seem like you're just friends to

me." I smiled. She added, "I can tell you like him,

and between me and you, he likes you too." I smiled and asked,

"Are you all friends?" She laughed and answered,

"God no, I'm Maverick's sister. I hate the rest of these guys, I just come for the free beer." I laughed, she smiled and got up. She jumped in the water.

As I sat there I could feel someone staring at me, I turned around and that guy was staring at me. It was like he'd been watching me the whole time. He walked over to me and sat down next to me, he had a beer in his hand and was obviously drunk. He said,

"Oh come on, just one drink. It won't hurt you." I said,

"No thanks." He grabbed my arm and asked,

"Why not?" I pushed him away from me, I stood up and walked towards the water, he followed me. He grabbed my wrist and asked, "why are you making me beg?" I pulled my arm away and yelled,

"Get away from me!" He gripped my arm even harder, he said,

"One drink, that's it!" I started to sweat, I was looking around waiting for someone to see. I yelled,

"I don't want a drink!" His breath smelled of alcohol, his mouth went close to my ear and whispered,

"Let's have some fun." I could feel his breath in my ear. He pulled out a bag of pills, some were crushed others were whole. I pulled my arm away and said,

"No!" Lainey heard me and she walked over to us. She asked,

"What's going on?" He said,

"We're just gonna go have some fun."

Lainey looked at me, she looked at my arm and him squeezing it. Lainey said, "let her go." He let my arm go, but stood beside and said,

"I just wanted to have some fun, you look like you would be fun." I could hear footsteps coming towards us. Maverick asked,

"What's going on?" Lainey answered,

"You need to get her outta here." He looks at me, I look down at my feet. Lainey said, "your scumbag friend was trying to get her drunk and high. He was squeezing her arm." I could see Maverick's face. His friend laughed and said,

"I just wanted some fun." Maverick nodded and punched him in the nose, my eyes got big. I asked,

"Should we stop this?" She laughed and answered,

"Good luck pulling him off, when someone hurts a person he cares about he goes insane." Lainey yelled, "alright boys that's enough!" Maverick had him on the ground, Lainey put her hand on Maverick's shoulder and said, "I think he learned his lesson." He got up and wiped his bloody nose. He asked,

"Are you okay?" I answered,

"The real question is, are you okay?" He answered,

"Never better." His knuckles are bloody, his nose is bleeding. He asked, "you wanna leave?" I answered,

"No, I'm good." He looked at me and said,

"We can leave if you want to." I shook my head and smiled, I answered,

"I'm fine." He looked at me, my eyes were glossy. He knew something was wrong, he could tell. He turned to Lainey and asked,

"Do you wanna ride with us?" She nodded and took the keys from Maverick. Lainey announced,

"You're not driving, you're still mad!" He laughed and put his arm around me, his knuckles bruised. Lainey looked miles ahead, we walked slowly to the car. I asked,

"You do that a lot?" He asked,

"Do what?" I answered,

"Fight? Do you fight a lot?" He smiled and answered,

"When it's necessary." I smiled, when we got to the car Lainey already started it, he opened the passenger side door, I crawled in and he crawled in the back. When is it necessary? What does that even mean? Lainey asked,

"Where are we going?" Maverick asked,

"Are you guys hungry?" Lainey laughed and answered,

"I don't third wheel, how about I drop y'all off at a restaurant and then come back later?" Maverick looked at me and smiled, I smiled. He said,

"Is that what you wanna do?" I smiled and nodded. Lainey squealed,

"That's so cute! Your first date!" We pulled up at a small diner just outside of town. She dropped us off and sped off, he put his arm around me.

We walked inside and sat at the counter, it was quiet, the diner was small. It reminded me of a coffee shop, it had little brown tables and a long brown counter. I was quiet, I was just thinking, thinking about what would happen when I go home. He asked,

"You okay?" I smiled and answered,

"Yeah, I'm okay." The whole time I could tell he was worried, I could tell that he knew something was wrong. I felt something hit my hair, I asked,

"Did you just throw a fry at me?" He laughed and answered,

"Yeah, I can tell something's wrong." I said,

"I'm fine, it wasn't that big of a deal. Your

friend was drunk, I know how people get when

they're drunk." He asked,

"Why are you so okay with it? He was

forcing himself on you!" I answered,

"I grew up around drunks, I know how it

feels to be scared, and vulnerable. I also know how

to take care of myself in that kind of situation. I am

okay." He could tell I was lying, but about which

part? He said,

"No one should have to go through that." He

puts his hand on mine, and he smiles. I smiled, I

took out my phone and checked the time 4:01, 4:01.

I could feel my chest get tight and my palms start to

sweat, I said,

"I have to go." I grabbed my sweater and walked out the door of the diner. He followed me out into the parking lot. He asked,

"What's the rush?" I answered,

"My father's gonna kill me!" I started to panic, he'll know I wasn't at school, he'll know where I was. He put his hand on my shoulder and said,

"It's okay! Just calm down, we'll figure something out!" I took a deep breath and said,

"It's okay, I'll figure something out." He followed me as I walked away, I turned around and said, "you go back inside and finish eating, I just have to go home." He said,

"I'll call Lainey, we'll take you home." I smiled, I said,

"I'm okay, I have to go." He cupped my face and kissed me. His lips brushing against mine, I pulled away and got into the cab. When I got home the house was quiet, but I knew it wouldn't stay that way.

~4~

My father was asleep on the couch, I knew he heard me come in. I went to my room and waited, waited for the questions. Waited for something to happen, waiting for the anger. Waiting for the storm, waiting for everything to come crashing down. I could hear him walking up the steps, I could hear his footsteps echoing.

As a child I memorized the way he walked, I knew what his footsteps sounded like, I knew when he would come into my room at night, I knew what was going to happen before it even did.

When he came in my room he stood in the doorway, he asked,

"Where have you been?" I answered,

"I went to lunch after school." He nodded and asked,

"With who?" I answered,

"A friend." He walked towards the bed and asked,

"What friend?" He closed the door behind him. I answered,

"Lainey, she's in my English class." He nodded, he laughed. He asked,

"Do you think I'm stupid?" I shook my head, his hand hit the wall. I jumped at the sound of his fist going through the wall. He yelled,

"Do you think I'm stupid?" I answered,

"No." Everything after that was a blur, I

woke up in my bed in a pool of my own blood. My

head was bleeding, broken ribs, bruises up and

down my body.

I could feel the pain in my ribs, everytime I

breathed there were shooting pains in my chest and

stomach, I could barely walk without feeling like

my insides were going to burst out.

I walked quietly to the bathroom and opened

the medicine cabinet. Searching for something,

anything. Ibuprofen, pain killers, something. I groan

in pain as I search the cabinet, I take a deep breath

but it hurts worse.

I took some Ibuprofen but nothing worked.

Today he was angry, tomorrow he'll be sad and it'll

keep going in a circle until one of us dies.

Eventually I fall asleep, or pass out, they both feel the same. Most of my life I've spent in this room, hiding from the monster outside of it. Yesterday I did something that I wanted. I was happy for a second.

Then again, happiness only lasts a second, but pain can last a lifetime. Life has its ups and downs, that's a given but sometimes the lows are too low to come back from. Sometimes it's better to give up than to keep fighting.

Sometimes it's easier to give up, sometimes it's okay to be selfish and do what you need to. I didn't go to school, I couldn't cover the bruises on my body. My father came in my room and said,

"Get up, I'm taking you somewhere." I asked,

"Where are we going?" He answered,

"Don't ask questions, let's go." I got out of bed and followed him to the car. We drove in silence but the grip he had on the steering wheel told me he was angry. I asked,

"Where are we going?" He yelled,

"Shut up! Just shut up!" He started swerving in between the lanes. He lost control and I could see the car going off the road. I looked over at him and the panic on his face was the last thing I saw.

I could remember going in and out of consciousness. In the ambulance I could see the paramedic but I couldn't say anything. I could feel my eyes get heavy and they were so heavy that I couldn't keep them open.

I could hear voices but I couldn't open my eyes, it was like that for days, day in and day out. Sunrise to sunset, I could hear the doctors, I could feel them but my eyes were like they were glued shut. I could hear my father talking to the doctors, I could hear all the lies he was telling them. I heard a familiar voice, I heard him. My father asked,

"Who are you?" He answered,

"A friend." My father asked,

"A friend? Listen if you don't mind I'd rather be alone with her." Maverick asked,

"Those bruises, they look old. Older than the bruises on her face. What are they from?" My father answered,

"Listen I don't know who you are, or what she told you but she has a condition, a disease. She has bipolar disease, I don't know what lies she told you but she tends to hurt herself. She doesn't remember hurting herself and tends to make lies about what happened." Maverick said,

"She didn't tell me anything." I could tell by his voice he was confused. Maverick asked, "the day we hung out she said you were gonna kill her, she said she was used to being around drunks." My father said,

"That's the disease talking, her mind makes things up and she doesn't even know it. Sometimes she gets other people involved, sometimes people believe her. I've learned over time to not believe anything she says." Maverick asked,

"Why wouldn't she tell me?" He answered,

"I don't think that she knows, I don't think her mind lets her process it." It went quiet, so did my mind. I could hear anything, I couldn't feel anything. I was nothing, I laid there as nothing. I couldn't feel anything, my body wasn't mine. It was like my thoughts and feelings just stopped. The whole world went quiet, everything was quiet, peaceful almost.

I woke up, it was a rush of confusion, I didn't know where I was and I couldn't remember anything past the age of seven, at least I think. I saw the doctor in the corner, I could see him slowly approach me. He smiled and asked,

"Do you know your name?" I shook my head, I couldn't form the words but I couldn't remember my name either. He smiled and added, "It's okay, it's normal to have some amnesia after a head injury." I nodded, then I saw him. I saw my father walk in, I remembered him. It was a switch in my brain that went off, it was like I sensed the danger by him just walking into the room. He smiled and asked,

"How you feeling?" I answered,

"I'm fine." He smiled and walked over to the doctor. I could hear them whispering. My father whispered,

"She has bipolar disease, she needs to be on medication." The worst thing about it is I couldn't remember if he was lying. The doctor nodded and walked over to the bed. The doctor asked,

"How are you feeling? Are you feeling manic?" I answered,

"I feel fine." He nodded and asked,

"Can you remember anything from the crash?" I answered,

"I only remember the tree, I could see the car going towards the tree and then everything went black." My father sat next to me and put his hand on mine. He said,

"Honey we've been over this, you and your mother are bipolar. I know you don't remember but we're gonna get you help." I nodded, I kept trying to think back but my mind went blank each time. The doctor announced,

"The amnesia should wear off in a couple of days, if it doesn't we may need to run more tests." My father nodded and asked,

"What kind of help can I get her with her bipolar disease?" The doctor answered,

"It depends on how bad it gets, we could send her to one of our facilities for 72 hours." My father asked,

"Can we do that now?" The doctor asked,

"Now? Has she shown any manic signs?" My father answered,

"No but it's better for her to get help

sooner." The doctor argued,

"Sir, I highly suggest that we let these first

few days play out." He yelled,

"I don't wanna wait! She needs help so

bring me the damn papers!" The doctor nodded and

left the room. I asked,

"What's gonna happen now?" He answered,

"We're gonna get you help." I asked,

"Can I see the papers?" He hesitated. I could

tell that he didn't have the papers. He answered,

"We've been over this, your mother took

them and put them somewhere before she died." I

said,

"She didn't die, she left." I couldn't

remember why, I couldn't remember why she left

but I'll remember eventually. The doctor came in

with a packet of papers and without skipping a beat my father signed them. Sending me off the psych ward, sending me somewhere that I could be silent and I could be gone.

~5~

Two nurses came into the room, and they gave my father discharge papers. I knew as soon as I was discharged he was going to drop me off. At this point I could only remember a couple things, everything was still so blurry and fuzzy.

I don't remember much before the crash, I can remember my father's grip on the steering wheel but as I try to remember more my mind goes blank. I got out of the bed, still sore, still in pain. I felt a rush to my head and memories started flowing, I felt like I was going to pass out.

I just saw images of my father, everytime he put his hands on me, Maverick and I, my mother leaving. All these memories came flooding back, I looked at my father.

He was still putting on the show of being a great dad, of trying to help his daughter because she had a disease. I took a deep breath and said,

"I'm not bipolar, mom was but I'm not. She didn't, she left because she couldn't handle your abuse anymore." The nurse stares at me and then back at my father. He asked,

"Do you think I would be able to stand here if I abused you?" I answered,

"Yeah, I do. Your brother's a cop, I told him everything as I stood on that bridge but he turned away. You've always had a way of protecting yourself and quite honestly I applaud you for that. I will not put up with your abuse anymore!" He said,

"Caitlyn, you're having an episode, and I'm going to get you help." He walk towards me, he grabbed my hand and I yelled,

"Don't touch me! Don't even come near me!" He nodded and asked,

"What are you gonna do now? You gonna tell people? Honey, they won't believe you. You just got your memories back, maybe you're confused." I yelled,

"I'm not confused!" I walk out the room, the nurses too stunned to speak. He didn't follow me, he knew I was right, he knew that he couldn't hide forever. I knew that eventually something would have to change, I knew that something would have to happen, I needed to escape. I walked home, hoping he wasn't there, I grabbed a bag and threw

clothes in it as fast as I could.

I couldn't handle it anymore, I couldn't take

it anymore. I knew that if I stayed, I would end up

dead. I left, I took my mom's old car and left. I

didn't know where to go but I needed to go

somewhere, somewhere far away.

I drove, it felt like I drove in a circle, it felt

like there was nowhere to go. Somehow I kept

going home, it's the only thing I've ever known.

His abuse was normal, it was another day, it was my

life.

We all grew up different, some have harder

lives than others but we've all been through things.

People say that there's heroes and villains but life

isn't that black and white. It's more complicated

and messy, sometimes the villains are actually the

heroes and the heroes turn out to be the villains. As humans, we like to find the good in people but sometimes it's not there.

I knew where I needed to go, I knew what I needed to do. I needed to talk to someone, I needed to talk to that one person. I knew where she was, we kept in touch over the years but it wasn't the same. I drove for hours until I got to her house.

I knocked twice, I debated just walking away. Was it worth seeing her again? Was a part of me mad at her for leaving me? Of course I was mad, I was so mad at first but I understood. I knew why she left, what I didn't understand, was why didn't she take me with her?

Why did she leave me behind? I can hear someone come to the door, I can hear the door knob turn. She opened the door, I could see the utter

shock on her face. I announced,

"Hi mom." She asked,

"What are you doing here?" I answered,

"I don't know." She stared at me, I didn't

know why I was here. At least I didn't want to

admit why I was there, I didn't want to admit that I

was saying goodbye, I didn't want to admit I was

angry.

I didn't want to admit that I hated her for

what she did, I didn't want to admit that I resented

her for leaving me with that man. She came outside

and closed the door. She said,

"It's not a good idea for you to be here." I

nodded. She added, "I'm a different person now,

I'm taking my meds, I have a family." I said,

"Yeah, you have a new family, I'm happy for you, but don't ever forget that you had a family! You had me, but in the end I guess I wasn't good enough!" I shake my head and walk off her porch. She announced,

"I'm sorry!" I walked towards her and yelled,

"You don't get to be sorry! You left me, you left me to deal with all his abuse! You can take your apology, I don't want it!" She asked,

"Will you ever forgive me?" I asked,

"Forgive you for what? Leaving me? Starting a new family? Standing there on your high horse asking me to forgive you? No I won't forgive you, and that's just something you have to live with." She nodded, I closed my eyes and stood there, I couldn't move for a second. My back facing her, I asked, "why didn't you take me?" When I opened my eyes a tear streamed down my face, my body felt heavy. She answered,

"When I left, I wasn't on my meds. I was only thinking about myself. I knew that if I came back for you he would kill me." I laughed and asked,

"Do you know how many times he tried to kill me? Do you know how many times I went to the ER?" She stayed quiet, I added, "do you know how many times I told someone? Everytime, every goddamn time no one believed me. Do you know how it feels to be called a bipolar freak show? Oh yeah, I'm bipolar now." She asked,

"What?" I answered,

"Yeah, I just woke up from a coma and just got my memories back, now I'm bipolar and they're trying to send me to a psych ward. I just came to

say goodbye." She asked,

"To say goodbye? Where are you going?" I

answered,

"Hell probably. Not yet, I have a couple

more stops to make but, I guess I'll see you in hell."

She walked towards me as I walked to the car. I

drove off, I had to make it believable. It killed me to

see her but I needed to, I needed to see her. I needed

to tell her how I felt.

~6~

It was hard seeing her again, there were a lot

of feelings that I had. I pulled over, my dad was

calling me. He left voicemails but I didn't listen to

them, there was no point. I knew that he would find

me if I stayed, I knew he would keep me here. I had

to see one last person, I had to see him.

I had to tell him the truth, he deserves the

truth. I drove to his house, it wasn't far from my

house. It was a small town, everyone knew

everyone. Everyone believed all the lies we all told.

Everyone believed whatever we said, they

believed each time I 'fell down the stairs' or 'I got

jumped' they believed each and every lie.

That was the problem, he was respected. No

one would believe a teenager, they would label it as

being *rebellious*. It was pointless to speak up, it was

pointless to stay. I knocked on his door, his sister

answered. She smiled and called her brother's

name. I got anxious as he walked towards the door.

He asked,

"What are you doing here?" I answered,

"I'm telling you the truth. After everything at the hospital you deserve that." He shut the door as he came outside, we sat on his porch swing. I began, "I'm not bipolar, my mother was but I'm not. My father is abusive, he abused my mother up until she left. He abused me once she left. Everything he told you are lies. You don't have to believe me but if you choose to believe him then I don't really have anything else to say." He asked,

"He abused you?" I answered,

"Abuses, but yes. Listen he told the doctors that I'm bipolar and they're looking for me. I just came to tell you the truth but I gotta get outta here." Maverick asked,

"Did you ever tell anyone? Like cops." I answered,

"I've told everyone, I've told teachers,

counselors, cops. No one believes the teenager.

Every time I told someone he almost killed me, so

don't do anything stupid." He asked,

"Why doesn't anyone believe you?" I

answered,

"My father's respected, he was the golden

child growing up, he was the person who could do

no wrong. His brother's a cop so I guess they

wouldn't think anything." He stood up and

exclaimed,

"This isn't right! He shouldn't just get away

with it!" I said,

"He already has, he's been getting away

with it for years." He said,

"It doesn't make sense, how do you have

your memories back?" I answered,

"I don't have all of them back, there's still holes." He asked,

"What holes?" I shrugged my shoulders, there were memories that I couldn't remember. I answered,

"I don't know, it's just all the fights we had, I can't really remember what they were about." He nodded and asked,

"You okay?" I answered,

"No." He wrapped his arms around me and said,

"It's gonna be okay." I took a deep breath and said,

"I gotta get outta here." He asked,

"Where are you gonna go?" I answered,

"I don't know, but I know I can't stay here."

A car pulled up, I recognized the car. I took a deep

breath and mumbled, "shit." He looked at me and
then back at the car. He asked,

"Is that?" I nodded, he grabbed my arm and
shook his head. I said,

"Stop, you're gonna make it worse." He got
outta the car and yelled,

"Caitlyn, get in the car!" I walked towards
the car and asked,

"You're stalking me now? What is it this
time? You gonna burn me with some cigarettes like
when I was ten? Or maybe with a lighter this time
like when I was thirteen." He yelled,

"Shut up and get in the car!" I shook my
head and said,

"I'm not getting in the car, you're drunk and
we're not getting in a car accident again." I could
feel Maverick walking behind me. He yelled,

"Don't move!" He pulled out a gun and pointed it at Maverick. I stood in front of him and said,

"Don't point it at him!" He placed the gun on my head and said,

"Get in the car!" The gun resting on my forehead, I shook my head and said,

"I'm not that scared little girl anymore, you don't scare me anymore." Maverick announced,

"Put the gun down!" I yelled,

"Maverick, just go inside!" My father locked eyes with me. I whispered, "just let him go inside." He nodded, Maverick said,

"I'm not leaving you out here!" My father looked at him and said,

"She just needs help, let me get her help!" I took a deep breath, my chest was starting to get tight, I could feel a lump in my throat. I asked,

"What do you wanna do?" My father answered,

"You need help, let me get you help!" I nodded and said,

"Okay, you have to put the gun down." He dropped the gun and a gunshot went off. The gun fell to the ground, I stood there, watching the gun fall. I could only focus on the gun, it was like the whole world around the gun was blurry. I took a deep breath, I heard Maverick running towards me,

I heard the leaves crunching as he stepped on them. I look down at the blood on my hands, the blood dripping through my fingers onto the leaves. I look down, the leaves more red than they were before.

The grass stained where the blood fell, it was quiet, I blocked out the noise and focused on the ground. Focused on the blood, there was a puddle, the blood fell from my leg. Maverick sat me on the floor and applied all his body weight to the whole in my leg. His parents and his sister swarmed around me. His mother was hysterical on the phone, his father bent down talking to me, I couldn't make out what he was saying. His voice sounded muffled, my focus still on the gun, my father's car was gone and so was he. Lainey throwing up in the house and Maverick still applying pressure, I start to feel light headed but if I closed my eyes I wondered if I would ever wake up again.

As the ambulance drove I heard them talking but it was muffled, it sounded like static behind a radio. I could feel Maverick's grip on my arm, he held my arm until we got to the hospital, they took me into surgery to remove the bullet. When they put me under everything went blank, there was nothing there, no thoughts.

It was like watching a blank TV screen, dark and nothing on it. When I woke up it was bright, the light was shining in my eyes. I tried to sit up but a sharp pain shot up my leg. I closed my eyes and laid back, Maverick was sleeping in the chair beside the bed. I smiled, I didn't wake him. He looked actually peaceful, he deserved it after today. I took a deep breath and watched him sleep. I saw someone come down the hallway, my father stood in the hallway. I said,

"Get out!" He raised his arms and said,

"I'm sorry." I yelled,

"You're sorry? You shot me!" He said,

"It was an accident!" Maverick woke up, he looked at me then at the door. He stood up and said,

"Get out." He walked towards my father and said, "now." My father left the room, Maverick walked back over to the bed and asked,

"How you feeling?" I answered,

"Like I got shot." I smiled, he smiled and asked,

"You hungry?" I answered,

"No, I'm good." Maverick announced,

"You have to eat something." I said,

"I will, you worry too much." He smiled and said,

"I gotta worry, you're my girlfriend." I smiled and said,

"Well, I think that you need to relax. I need my boyfriend to be calm." He smiled and said,

"I'll be calm when we're out of here." I smiled and said,

"Your parents must hate me." I laughed, he laughed with me. He said,

"I don't think they know you enough to hate you." I laughed and said,

"I think getting shot in your front yard is a deal breaker for a parent." He smiled and the room went quiet. I've had a hard life, some people don't see me as a person, they see me as damaged goods.

I looked down at my face and my eyes lingered.

Maverick cupped my face and said,

"We'll figure it out." I nodded. He got up
and kissed me on the forehead, he left the room and
I just sat in the hospital bed. I just sat there and
thought, how could I let it get this bad? How could I
let him do this?

There's a lot that I had to put up with. He'll
alway be my father, he'll always be the one who
raised me but that's what I was scared of. Aren't we
all influenced by the people who raised us? Isn't our
whole lives influenced by the people who raised us?

I fell asleep but I didn't dream, my mind
was blank. There was nothing to think about,
nothing to worry about. I was in a hospital, nothing
would happen. I didn't have to deal with reality
until tomorrow. Right now, I could just sleep. I

woke up to a nurse putting a IV in my arm, I winced

as the needle went into my arm. She whispered,

"I'm sorry." I asked,

"What is that?" She answered,

"Just a painkiller." I pushed her hand away

and said,

"No, I'd rather not." She looked confused, I

added, "my father's addicted to drugs, addiction

runs in my family, I don't wanna risk it." She

nodded, I've never drank alcohol, I've never taken

any drugs. One pill or one drink can lead to an

addiction and I've seen what addictions do to

people. I sat up on the bed and my eyes filled with

tears, I covered my mouth as I sobbed. I didn't want

to wake Maverick up, I just started thinking, how

could I just jump into a relationship? I don't even

know myself, don't even know who I am. How am I

supposed to be in a relationship when I don't even know what I want?

My whole life I always worried about everyone else, I never stopped to think about myself. I needed to think about what I wanted, about what I needed. I needed to step back, I needed to take a deep breath and realize what I wanted. I needed to focus on myself. Set someone free, but if they love you they'll come back.

Maverick woke up, my eyes were puffy and red. He looked at me, the look on his face said it all. He was scared but concerned, I could see his eyes looking up and down my body, looking for blood. I whispered,

"I don't think I can do this." He looked at me and I could tell that his heart broke as I said those words. He asked,

"Really?" I could hear his voice breaking. I answered,

"I don't think it's realistic for us to jump into something so quickly." He nodded, I took a deep breath and added, "I think I need to find myself before I think about a relationship." He nodded and said,

"Okay." He asked, "that's it?" I answered,

"I don't know, I don't want it to be but if we jump into something we're not gonna work. We're gonna hate each other." He whispered,

"I could never hate you." I smiled, how could he not hate me? How could he not hate me even though I hate myself? I asked,

"How do you know? How do you know that you won't hate me?" He answered,

"Because when I look at you, Caitlyn, when I look at you there's nothing I'd rather be doing. There's nowhere in this world I'd rather be, there's no one in the world I'd rather be with. It's me and you, always." I asked,

"But how do you know?" He answered,

"I don't, it's not like a fact. It's a feeling! It's how I feel, I know how I feel and I wanna be with you!" I cupped his face and whispered,

"I wanna be with you too, but I don't know if I can. I don't wanna hold you back." He whispered,

"Get outta your head, we wanna be together." I pulled away and said,

"I won't be the one to hold you back, we're sixteen. You have your whole life ahead of you!" He mumbled,

"I wanna spend it with you!" I take a deep

breath and whispered,

"I think you should go."

~8~

I watch as he walks out the room, trying to

fight back tears as he gets closer to the door. I

wanted to yell for him not to go but like they say, if

you love them, set them free. When I hear the door

shut I close my eyes and let the tears roll down my

face. I took a deep breath and standing in the

doorway was my father. He said,

"Your guardian has to sign the discharge

papers." I mumbled,

"Just kill me now." He closed the door

behind him and said,

"I'm gonna sign you out and then you have seventy two hours to get outta here. If you don't you'll go to a psych ward. Do you understand?" I laughed and asked,

"Oh, you've gone soft." He said,

"Seventy two hours." I nodded, he opened the door and came back with a clipboard. He signed the papers, and I left. My foot in a boot, walking down the street.

Walking to get my car from his house, I debated on saying goodbye but it felt like we already did. Saying goodbye again would just cause more pain. I got to my car, my keys were in the bag of my stuff the hospital gave me.

I was hoping I didn't see him but before I could get in my car Lainey came outside and ran to me. She hugged me and said,

"I'm so glad you're okay!" I smiled, I

opened my car door. She asked, "what are you

doing?" I answered,

"I'm leaving." She asked,

"Where are you going?" I answered,

"Anywhere but here." She asked,

"You're just gonna leave?" I answered,

"I don't have a choice." She asked,

"So that's it? You're just gonna leave him?

After everything he's done for you!" I yelled,

"Do you honestly think I wanna leave? I

don't wanna leave him but I don't have a choice! I

need him to be successful! I can't get in the way of

his future!" Lainey laughed, I could see the anger

on her face. She yelled,

"Then stay!" I exclaimed,

"It's not that easy! Not for me!" She said,

"I doubt your life is that hard!" I could see

Maverick in the front yard, he yelled,

"Lainey, stop!" I laughed and yelled,

"You have no idea what I've been through!"

Lainey looked at Hunter, he shook his head at her.

She yelled,

"Come on Caitlyn, tell us what you've been

through!" I clench my jaw, I close my eyes hoping

when I open them it would be over. When I opened

my eyes she raised her eyebrows. I asked,

"You really wanna know? I have been

burned, cut, beaten. My father is a drunk who

wanted to get his relief by his daughter! He shot me,

that was the least painful." I walked closer and

added, "don't for a second think you got it hard

because I can promise you, I've been through

everything. I've experienced everything you can

think of!" She couldn't look me in the eyes. She whispered,

"Everything?" I answered,

"Even what you're thinking of." I knew what she was thinking of. I knew what she was asking, I knew what Maverick was thinking too. I took a deep breath and I could hear Maverick walking towards me. Lainey whispered,

"I'm sorry, I didn't know." I took a deep breath and backed up. Maverick was walking towards me, he could tell that I felt cornered. He just grabbed me and pulled me into his arms. I felt safe as I heard his heartbeat. He whispered,

"It's okay." I sobbed in his arms, he hugged me tight, tight enough where I didn't want to let go. He ran his fingers through my hair as I sobbed, Lainey stood there as we hugged. It felt like everyone and everything stopped and the world was finally quiet. I pulled away and said,

"I have seventy two hours to leave or he'll come looking for me." Maverick shook his head and said,

"No, you can't leave!" I said,

"Maverick, if I don't leave he'll send me to a psych ward and I don't wanna go through that again!" Maverick eyes got wide and asked,

"Again?" I took a deep breath and answered,

"This isn't the first time that he used the bipolar lie, this isn't the first time I've been in the hospital and this isn't the first time I was threatened with a gun. He never actually shot me before but here we are." He asked,

"Then let me come with you. Can I come with you?" I cupped his face and with tears in my eyes I answered,

"We both know you can't do that." He asked,

"Why not?" His voice breaking as he spoke. I answered,

"Because you have a life here, you have people who care about you here. Your whole life is here." I took my hands off his cheek and wiped his tears away. I smiled and said, "I need you to be the best version of yourself and you coming with me wouldn't give you a chance." He grabbed my hands and kissed them. He asked,

"Where are you going?" I answered,

"Wherever the road takes me." I smiled and took the necklace from around my neck, the angel pendant falling into the hand. I took his hand and placed the necklace inside of it. I closed his hand shut and said, "don't worry, you'll see me again. Maybe not for a while but, if you love someone they'll come back." I smiled and said, "just don't forget about me, okay?" He answered,

"I'll never forget you, I'll remember everything." I smiled and turned around. I walked to my car and I could feel him staring at me as I walked away. I didn't want to walk away but it was the only option, it gave us what we both needed even if we didn't want that to be true.

We both needed to find ourselves and put ourselves first. We needed to be apart so when we finally found eachother again we would know what we wanted. I got in my car and I looked out the window at him one last time, at least for now.

I started the car and pulled off, I felt like I was leaving a part of me behind but this town was never my home, but he was. He made this town worth living in, the more I spent time with him the more I realized that he was special, he was different than everyone else.

Being near him made everything seem okay, it made everything seem less important and less heartbreaking. He made everything easier, he made everything better.

I drove for what seemed like hours, I didn't really have a set plan on where I was going. As I drove through the wooded area, for as far as I could see was trees. The sunset made the trees look beautiful, the roads seemed reflective of the pink sky.

I stopped at a gas station after driving for

two hours, I needed a phone charger. I left in a

hurry without anything really. I have my wallet but

nothing else. I walked in and the smell of beer and

plastic hit me as I walked further. The gas station

was bright, it seemed out of place for the darkness

outside. The man smiled at me, he asked,

"Is that everything for you?" I answered,

"Yeah, that's everything." He smiled and

nodded, he kept staring at me as I stood there

counting my money. I handed him a ten dollar bill,

he looked at my hand as he handed it to him. His

eyes ventured up to my face. He just kept smiling at

me. His eyes ventured back down to my chest, I

noticed but I stayed quiet. He handed me my change

and grabbed my hand as he put the change in my

hand. I pulled my hand away and asked, "are you serious?" He smiled and answered,

"Have a good day." I rolled my eyes and walked out of the store. The door slammed behind me, I could hear the bells ring as the door shut. I took a deep breath, I started the car and drove off.

I drove for what seemed like hours, I was out of town but it still felt like I wasn't far enough. I knew he would find me, it doesn't matter how far I went. I was waiting for the seventy two hours to be up, I was waiting for him to be waiting for me. It was like a never ending cycle, like a cat hunting for a mouse most of the time it ends badly.

I continued to drive until I was falling asleep at the wheel. I pulled over and looked for the closest motel. The closest motel was Route 66 Inn, I'm in Texas but it still doesn't seem far enough. It doesn't matter how far I go, he'll find me. He's always had

a way of finding people. I check into the motel and

my phone rings. I answered,

"Hello?" The voice said,

"Dad overdosed." My brother's voice

cracked. I asked,

"Is he okay?" He answered,

"It's not looking good." I take a deep breath

and asked,

"Am I supposed to care? After everything

he's done to us? You got out! I didn't!" He said,

"He's still our father!" I yelled,

"What? You want me to come back to

comfort you? To go to a funeral and listen to

everyone say that he was a great man?" He

answered,

"No, I want you to come back for me! I wanna know everything that happened while I was gone! I wanna know why you never talk about me and treat me like I don't exist!" I yelled,

"Because you got out! You left, you left me! Your world kept spinning and mine stopped!" He stayed quiet for a while. I added, "do you know what it's like to have your father come into your room while you're sleeping? Do you know how it feels to have your insides curl up every time you see him." He asked,

"Can you please come back?" I answered,

"I just left, I just ended my role in that town. Now you're asking me to come back? That's pretty damn selfish." I hung up the phone, I threw it. I covered my mouth as I sobbed. Everytime I thought about my father, my insides curled up, it felt like I was on fire inside of me. I took a deep breath, should I go back? I just left not even eight hours ago, if I go back what would happen? If I go back I will have to relive everything, if I go back everyone will tell me what a great person he was. No one saw what happened in our house, no one would even care.

If I go back will I be happy? Do I even want to go back? I lay down, for the first time in a long time I don't have to worry about him coming into my room. I don't have to worry about holding my breath until it's over. I don't have to worry about anything, but if I go back I'll be the same scared little girl I always was.

As soon as I laid down I went to sleep, my mind was at ease. The question is still unanswered, will I go back? Will I go back for my brother? How could I go back? How could I just go back with everything that happened?

When I woke up I realized that I couldn't take my anger out on my brother, no matter how much it hurt. He got out and I was glad he did but it still hurts that he left me. I had to be there not for my father but for him.

I got in my car and drove back to Oklahoma. I considered turning around but my brother needed me and I needed him too. I drove for five hours, five long hours until I pulled up to my house. I saw my brother on the front porch.

~10~

I could see he was crying, I stood in front of him. I walked past him and walked in the house, he cried for the father that put us through hell. He cried for the man who hurt him in ways that no one could imagine. I got a beer from the fridge, I opened it and took a quick drink. He came inside and said,

"You don't drink, you've never drank before." I tilted the beer back into my mouth and said,

"First time for everything I guess." He shook his head and walked back outside. I asked, "So when I drink it's wrong? But when he does it and gets violent it's fine?" He asked,

"What happened to you?" I yelled,

"I got abused! That's what happened, at the ripe age of six I had to drag his drunk ass in the house and get beat when he woke up! I grew up, that's what happened!" He yelled,

"Don't tell me about growing up!" I laughed and yelled,

"Oh please, you were the golden boy! You were the one who could do no wrong! You got a full ride to harvard! You wanna know what I got? An abortion at 12, so please don't talk to me about how you had it so rough!" He shook his head and said,

"Our dad is dying!" I exclaimed,

"No, your dad is dying!" I walked towards him and yelled, "your dad!" I walked out the house and got back in my car. I hit the steering wheel until my knuckles were bleeding, I took a deep breath and yelled, I yelled as loud as I could. I closed my eyes as I rested my head on the car seat. I couldn't understand how after everything he did to me, after everything he did to us, how could he still call him dad? I got out of my car and yelled, "who supported you when you came out? I did. He was ready to send you to conversion therapy!" He said,

"He didn't understand!" I yelled,

"Are you really that dumb? You've never been stupid but if you can't see him for who he truly is, you're just plain dumb." He answered,

"He loved us!" I answered,

"He loved you, he loved you like a son! He loved me like I was an object he could play with!" I looked him in the eye, tears falling down both of our faces. I took a deep breath and said, "at least he treated one of us like a person." As I walked back to my car he yelled,

"You're different." I shrugged my shoulders and said,

"Maybe I am." I got back in my car and pulled off. I went to the hospital, the only hospital in our small town. I went to the front desk and asked, "hi, can you tell me what room John Myers is in?" She asked,

"What's your relationship to the patient?" I answered,

"Daughter." She nodded and said,

"He's in room 218, down the hall to the left." I smiled and walked towards the room. As I entered the room I saw him lying in the bed, he seemed lifeless and motionless. He wasn't dead but a part of me wishes he was. I took a deep breath and sat beside the bed, tears fell down my face just thinking about everything over the years. I said,

"You know growing up I thought that was love, I thought that you hurting me was love. But that wasn't love because I know what love feels like and it's quite the opposite." I took a deep breath, my voice shaking. I got closer to the bed and said,

"what you did to me made me stronger so I guess I

should say thank you. I guess I should thank you for

being an abusive piece of shit. But I'm so angry at

myself for actually caring if you live or die, I'm

angry that I still care." I stood up and as I left the

room I said, "I hope you rot in hell." I left the room,

I was angry and upset but most of all I was

hurt. I still care about him and maybe I always will

but he hurt me in so many ways, I shouldn't care

about him. I don't want to care about him but a part

of me is that little girl waiting for him to stop

drinking and become my knight in shining armor,

that little girl is waiting for him to stop being the

dragon keeping her in the castle but here we are,

still stuck in the castle.

I got back in my car and looked back at my knuckles, they were raw and still bloody. I tried so hard to leave him alone but I needed to talk to him, I needed to be next to him. I needed to see him and I knew that when I left he was crushed but right now I don't even know what I'm going to do. Am I going to leave again?

There's nothing making me leave again, there's nothing to be afraid of anymore. I drove to his house, it felt weird being back. It felt like I wasn't supposed to be here, after I left not even forty eight hours ago.

I took a deep breath as I walked to his door, I debated turning around and walking back to my car but I didn't want to. I knocked twice and as soon as I saw him I bursted into tears. He looked down at my hands and asked,

"What happened?" I couldn't form any words, he hugged me and I cried harder. It felt like my world was crashing down but being in his arms made everything worth it. I answered,

"My dad's dying and I'm crying, why am I crying?" Maverick hugged me tighter and asked,

"Why are you back?" I pulled away and answered,

"I came back for my brother but he's on my father's side, it's like he never did anything wrong!" He grabbed my arms and pulled me into his arms, he said,

"It's okay, we'll get through it." I whispered,

"I'm sorry." He shook his head and said,

"Don't do that, don't apologize. Your father tormented you your whole childhood, you didn't have a choice." I took a deep breath and wiped my face. I smiled and said,

"I guess I just can't stay away." He smiled and said,

"You know you're supposed to run away from a fire, not into it." I smiled and said,

"Not my style." We both laughed, this is something that will always stick with me, sitting on the porch in the middle of a crisis and being able to laugh. I took a deep breath and mumbled, "what am I gonna do?" He answered,

"We're gonna go to your house and pack a bag for you, you're gonna stay here." I laughed and said,

"Yeah I don't think your parents will be too thrilled with that." He nodded and said,

"Then I'll pack a bag and go to your house."
I laughed and said,

"Yeah that's definitely not a good idea." He
smiled and put his arm around me. He asked,

"Are you gonna leave again?" I could hear
the sadness in his voice. I answered,

"I don't know." He whispered,

"Please don't leave again." I smiled and
buried my head into his shoulder.

~11~

I took a deep breath, I debated not going
home but the whole reason I was here was for my
brother. I said,

"I have to go home, I have to be there for
him." He nodded and stood up, he started walking

behind me. I asked, "what are you doing?" He answered,

"I'm coming with you." I shook my head and asked,

"Do you think that's a good idea? I mean my brother is just like my father and I don't want you to get caught up in that." He grabbed my shoulders and said,

"Hey, I'm coming." I nodded, he held his hand out and I gave him my keys. My knuckles had dried blood on them, my steering wheel stained red. He drove in silence, I was used to silence. Silence was good, silence was peaceful and silence was normal. He broke the silence, he turned the radio on and turned it almost all the way up, the windows were down and my hair was blowing all over the place. Maybe this was better than silence, maybe silence isn't so good.

He smiled at me, my mind was out the window. When we pulled up to my house my brother sat on the step, this time with three empty beer bottles beside him. I take a deep breath as I get out of the car, Maverick follows. My brother yelled,

"Cait, I didn't think you were coming back." His words slur as they leave his mouth, he stumbles as he walks towards me. I take a step back bumping into Maverick, jumping as he grabs me. I close my eyes and take a deep breath, reminding myself where I am. I asked,

"How many did you drink?" He laughs as he said,

"Four." I mumbled,

"Shit." Maverick whispers,

"What?" I answered,

"Three beers for him is the max, after four he gets violent." I walk towards my brother Maverick walking behind me. My brother said,

"Well this seems familiar." I announced,

"Ian, you need help. Let me help you, we can go inside and I'll help you to your room." Ian yelled,

"You help me? Funny, I needed you today and you weren't there!" I yelled,

"Ian, I'm not gonna keep having this same fight!" He yelled,

"Our father is dying!" I could see the tears on his face, they seemed to follow from the moonlight. I yelled,

"Your father is dying! Ian, he stopped being my father, the second mom left and you know that!"

He shook his head as he walked towards me, I felt small around him, he reminded me too much of my father. He grabbed my wrists and pulled me closer, I could smell the alcohol on his breath. Maverick walked closer, Ian yelled,

"After everything he did for you." I exclaimed,

"He didn't do anything for me, just to me!" He pushed me on the ground, Maverick pulled me up and said,

"We need to go!" I shook my head and said,

"I'm fine. He needs help!" Maverick said,

"Caitlyn, if you keep letting your family control you, they're gonna destroy you." I knew he was right, I nodded. Ian yelled,

"So just like that? You're just like mom!" I walked towards him and yelled,

"Don't ever say I abandoned you! You are the problem here, you know that we can't drink because both of our parents are alcoholics and you just ignored that! If I'm like mom, then you're just like dad!" He took a step towards us and said,

"You know at one point he loved you!" I yelled,

"I don't doubt that but in what way?" He asked,

"What does that even mean?" I answered,

"If I was his daughter then he wouldn't have come into my room at night! If I was his daughter then he wouldn't have hit me! If I was his daughter he wouldn't have burned me with cigarettes!" I took a deep breath and walked to the car, I couldn't do it anymore, I didn't want to have to explain myself every single day. I got in the car and Maverick

followed, we drove back to his house in silence.
When we pulled up to his house he got out of the
car, I stayed in the car.

I felt like I couldn't move, it felt like my
legs were paralyzed. I rubbed my face and took a
deep breath, I could see my breath inside the car.
My phone goes off almost every five minutes, my
brother texting me. Maverick comes back to the car
and sits in the driver's seat, he sits there and stares
at me. He asked,

"Where to now?" I answered,

"Hell hopefully." I laugh, he stays quiet. I
close my eyes and rest my head back on the seat. He
asked,

"Does that happen a lot?" I asked,

"What?" He answered,

"Your brother getting violent?" My eyes were still closed. I answered,

"Almost every time he comes home. He's gay and our father never supported him. He started drinking when he was sixteen. I was twelve and I supported him but a grown man didn't." Maverick shifted in his seat, I could hear his body moving against the leather seats. He asked,

"Do you know if he's gonna live?" I opened my eyes and looked at Maverick. I asked,

"Should I care?" He shook his head. I added, "it doesn't look good, but the bastard will probably pull through just to make my life hell." My phone rang, I ignored it. It rang again, and again, and again. By the fourth time I answered. I yelled, "what do you want, Ian?" I could hear his raspy voice, like he'd been crying. He answered,

"He's dead." I closed my eyes and hung up the phone. Why was I so upset? Why did I care? Maverick asked,

"What's wrong?" I answered,

"He's dead." Maverick put his arm around me and asked,

"Are you okay?" I nodded but tears fell from my face. He hugged me tighter and kissed my head. I took a deep breath and wiped my tears. I called Ian back and said,

"Ian, you need to sober up. I'll be over in the morning." He hung up, I needed him to be sober, I needed him thinking straight. Maverick asked,

"Are you going home?" I nodded and answered,

"He sounds upset, quite honestly I don't trust him alone right now." Maverick nodded and asked,

"Do you want me to come with you?" I shook my head and answered,

"I think it's better if you don't." He nodded and kissed me on the cheek, he got out of the car and I switched seats. I drove to my house and my brother was still sitting on the porch. I got out of the car and sat next to him. We sat there for a little while, just staring into the yard. I took a deep breath and asked, "did you go to the hospital yet?" He nodded, he stood up and went inside.

I tried to remember anything good about my father, but there wasn't much there. He was a bad person, he was a bad father, a bad husband, a bad drunk.

When I was four he took me to a park, I remember falling and he told me to stand up and shake it off. I remember his smile as he said it, he actually smiled. He wasn't always a bad father, there was a point where he was good but most of the time the good doesn't outweigh the bad.

~12~

I stood up, and looked around. This house, these memories, they were a part of me and I know that I'll never forget them but a part of me wishes they weren't there. I'll remember everything, I'll remember the times he came into my room, I'll remember the first time he burned me with a cigarette, and I'll remember how he made me feel.

We'll always carry our past, it doesn't matter how long ago it was, it doesn't matter how painful it was. Everyone has a past and everyone has gone through something, and if you're thinking right now that you haven't, you're lying to yourself.

We all go through something, whether it's a breakup, a divorce, abuse, substance abuse, sexual abuse, a toxic household, or just a hard time. We all go through things, stop comparing your traumas to other people.

I take a deep breath and go inside, I feel nauseous and my hands are shaking. Being in this house after he's gone feels different. The house isn't as dark as I remember, it's not as depressing as I remember it. I walk to my room and as I walk up the stairs I could feel all these memories rushing through me. I can see me at all ages running up these stairs, I could hear the footsteps as I saw myself running up the stairs.

I see a six year old me in a dress running up the steps laughing and giggling. Then I see myself at thirteen running up the stairs with blood rushing down my face. It was like I was right there watching from the outside. As I stood on the stairs it felt like I was right there. It was like I was standing at the top of the stairs watching myself.

I got chills and everything went dark. I could feel myself fall to the ground. It was black and I tried to open my eyes but I couldn't open them. It felt like I wasn't in my own body, it was just nothing.

I woke up in a hospital bed, I didn't know what happened but my head was throbbing. I touched my head and sat up, Maverick smiled at me. I asked,

"What happened?" He touched my hand and answered,

"You're okay, you're just dehydrated. Your brother brought you in and then he called me." I nodded and asked,

"Where's Ian?" He answered,

"He went home to sober up." I nodded and laid my head back on the pillow. I asked,

"How long was I out?" He answered,

"About an hour." I took a deep breath and nodded, the only thing I could think about was Ian and how alike him and our father were. I said,

"I came here the other day, I came to see my father and he was in the room where I was born. Room 218, I remember in a baby book my mother had. She took a picture of the sign on the wall, she took a picture of the room number." I smiled thinking back to when I was born, they were happy.

He was happy, he wasn't an alcoholic, he wasn't a

drug addict, he was my dad. Maverick asked,

"You were born here?" At that moment I

realized that we don't know anything about each

other, we just jumped into something when we

don't even know each other. I asked,

"What are we doing?" He looked around

and answered,

"We're sitting in a hospital." I shook my

head asked,

"No, what are *we* doing?" He answered,

"I don't know." I put my head back on the

pillow and looked at the ceiling. I said,

"We don't even know each other, we don't

know what we want or who we wanna be." He

asked,

"Who does Caitlyn Myers wanna be?" I

laughed and answered,

"I don't even know, at seven I wanted to be

a model and at fourteen I wanted to die. There

wasn't much room for thinking about the future."

He took a deep breath and said,

"I wanna be a doctor." I smiled and looked

up at him. I asked,

"What's stopping you?" He answered,

"Nothing." He looked at the door, I looked

down at the floor. He walked out and closed the

door behind him, he knocked twice and then opened

it back up. I asked,

"What are you doing?" He smiled and

answered,

"We're starting over." He stuck his hand out and said, "Maverick, pleasure to meet you again." I smiled and took his hand. I announced,

"Caitlyn Myers, hi again." We smiled and laughed, we talked about what we wanted. We talked about who we are and who we wanted to become. We talked for hours and it was great but soon enough we had to go back to reality. I had to face the fact that my father was dead and I would have to go to a funeral where everyone would talk about what a great person he was.

That would never change, everyone saw him for who he wanted to be. No one saw his flaws, no one saw his mistakes. They saw what he wanted them to see. Maverick asked,

"You ready to go?" I nodded, I got out of the bed, I still had my own clothes on. We left and went back to my house. I saw Ian inside, I could see

him through the window. He sat on the couch

looking through family albums. I said,

"You should go, you have school

tomorrow." He asked,

"Are you gonna be okay?" I nodded and he

walked home, I watched as he walked home. I

walked in the house, I sat on the couch next to him.

I watched as he flipped through the laminated

pages. He asked,

"You okay?" His eyes stayed on the book. I

answered,

"No." He nodded and closed the book, he

mumbled,

"I'm sorry." I took a deep breath and walked

to the window. I stared at the moon, it was

beautiful, it was full. The moon reminded me that

sometimes our beauty is hidden, sometimes we hide ourselves, we hide ourselves to protect ourselves. Most of the time we hide ourselves from the ugly truth, or sometimes we hide ourselves from reality. I asked,

"What are we gonna do?" He asked,

"About what?" I rolled my eyes. I asked,

"Who's planning the funeral?" He answered,

"The church volunteered to let us have it there, they said he deserves a proper funeral." I laughed and said,

"Because they know him so well." Ian took a deep breath and asked,

"Can we not do this? Can we not fight about him anymore?" I laughed, he didn't want to accept the fact that our father was horrible. I asked,

"When's the funeral?" He answered,

"Tomorrow." I nodded and stood up, as I walked to the stairs he asked, "are you gonna be there?" I answered,

"I don't know." I walked up to my room and I sat on the edge of the bed. I looked around the room and I thought of the little girl who used to sleep in here. She was so full of light, she didn't know how to react to her father. She was scared and hurt, when she looked at herself in the mirror she saw herself. When I was ten I started to see a disgusting human being, how things change over the years. At six I was a princess, at ten I was disgusting. My father made me into something, he made me feel like it was my fault. He made me feel dirty and like I wasn't worth anything, he made it my fault.

Now I have to sit in a room full of people saying what a great person he was and I'm supposed to stay quiet. As if I wasn't hurt or taken advantage of my whole childhood. I lay on the bed and I remember being the first time.

The first time he came into my bed, he opened my door and I was half asleep. I closed my eyes and pretended to be asleep, almost all kids pretend to be asleep and hide their phones under their pillow because they're afraid to get yelled at.

At first he sat on the edge of my bed and I could feel his eyes on me. Then he laid next to me and put his hand on thigh and his hand kept going up. I held my breath, I held my breath until it was over. I didn't know what was happening, I didn't know what sex was.

When he left I jumped out of my bed and put a chair against my door. My sheets were stained red with blood, I didn't know why. I didn't know what happened, I couldn't figure out what happened. I took the sheets off my bed and threw them in the hamper and I changed my clothes. That night I went to sleep but woke up three times from nightmares.

Tonight, I went to sleep and I didn't have a nightmare for the first time in a long time. I felt better knowing he wasn't here, somehow I felt safer but it still hurt being here.

~13~

I didn't want to wake up, I didn't want this day to be real. I debated not going to the funeral, what would happen if I didn't? The real question is,

116

what would happen if I did? If I went and would have to listen to these people, listen to people who didn't even know him, listen to them reminisce over all the good times when they weren't real.

My brother knocked on my door, he creeped in slowly. A glass of water in one hand and a bottle of Advil in the other. He smiled and said,

"I'm thinking you're gonna need this for today." I smiled and asked,

"Is this a peace offering?" He laughed and sat down next to me. He answered,

"Kinda, yeah." I took the advil and said,

"Promise me that we're in this together." He smiled and nodded. I shook my head and added,

"you have to say it!" He groaned and mumbled,

"I promise." I nodded, I took three Advil and drank the water. I took a deep breath and asked,

"What time is this stupid funeral?" He looked down at his watch and answered,

"In an hour." I flung my head back and groaned, he laid across the bed and asked,

"Why did we let him destroy us?" I laughed and answered,

"I am too sober for this conversation." We laughed and for the first time we were realizing that it was just him and I. I sat up and announced, "I think it's time to get ready." He asked,

"Is your boyfriend coming?" I laughed and asked,

"Do I really wanna put him through the pain of all the lies that will be told today?" Ian smiled and answered,

"The way I see it, it'll be pure entertainment." I laughed and said,

"I missed this. Us, I missed us." He smiled and stood up. He took a deep breath and announced, "Our hour just turned into forty minutes, chop chop." I took a deep breath as I picked through my closet. It hasn't been updated since my emo phase at thirteen, plenty of black dresses to choose from. I chose one that had lace up top and came just above my knees, it was his least favorite, it seemed right to wear. I looked at myself in the mirror, my hair matched the dress almost the same color. I didn't expect to wear this dress to a funeral.

For a minute it felt wrong, for a minute I looked in the mirror and asked myself, why am I doing this? Why should I even go? I closed my eyes and collected myself, I was only doing this for Ian. That's what I told myself but it wasn't true, I needed this to be over, I needed him to be gone.

I knocked on Ian's door, seeing him in a suit

took me back to his graduation. He looked so much

like our father that it hurts everytime I look at him.

When he talks I can separate them, he's so full of

light and passion, he's flawed but everyone is. I

asked,

"Are you ready to go?" He shook his head

and said,

"I can't figure out this stupid tie!" I smiled

and walked towards him. I said,

"Dad couldn't do it either, he made me

learn." I smiled as I tied it. I dusted off his

shoulders and added, "see, easy." He looked at me

and said,

"I'm sorry." I smiled as my eyes filled with

tears. I hated him, I hated him for what he did to me

but he's still my father. I feel like he'll alway be

there, he'll alway be in the back of my mind. He'll

always be in the back of my mind whispering,

you'll never be good enough, no one will ever love

you.

When you're seven, those words stick and

they'll alway be there. Like a song stuck in your

head and sing it when you're trying to fall asleep or

trying to do homework. It'll always be there, it'll

creep up on you. I smiled and asked,

"Shall we?" He wrapped his arm around

mine and nodded. He drove and I kept my head out

the window, like always. I admired the outside

because it didn't matter where you were, the outside

would always be there and always beautiful in some

way. Ian said, "you should call your boyfriend." I

shrugged and asked,

"I don't know if I want him to be there, our dad spread so many lies, what if he doesn't believe me?" Ian answered,

"He will, I know he will just by the way he looks at you." I smiled and took out my phone. I took a deep breath and I called him. It went straight to voicemail. I said,

"I'm on the way to my father's funeral and I don't know what's gonna happen, so call me back when you get this." Ian laughed and asked,

"That's all you got?" I laughed and answered,

"Shut up." He shook his head and asked,

"Why do you do that?" I asked,

"Do what?" He answered,

"Everytime you start to get close to someone, you shut down. Everytime, you just shut down." I nodded, he was right. I've always pushed people away because it was the only thing I knew how to do. I answered,

"People tend to leave." He nods and keeps his eyes on the road, I wasn't just talking about him. Our mother left too and that was something I could never forget.

When we pulled up at the church I didn't want to get out of the car. Ian opened my door and by the look on his face I could tell he didn't want to go in either. I take a deep breath and whispered,

"We got this." One step at a time, one step closer to seeing all the lies unfold because I will not let him get away with lying any longer then he already has.

~14~

As we walk in there seems to be at least

thirty maybe forty people already seated. Ian grips

my arm, he's nervous and upset. We walked over to

his casket, seeing him lay there lifeless. A part of

me wanted to hit him and a part of me wanted to

yell at the top of my lungs.

Everyone came over to us, they said *I'm*

sorry for your loss, he was a great man. They were

all lies, we sat down but Ian was the one who had to

speak. Ian took a deep breath and he began,

"Today we mourn John Myers, tomorrow

we move on. My father, our father was a man of

many faces to say the least. I like to believe that the

past is the past but regardless of the situation, it

follows us. He will always follow us, maybe not

physically but mentally and spiritually if you

believe in that." I scan the room, and people are crying. I couldn't believe how many people he's lied to. Ian sat down and I stood up. I walked to the front of the room and announced,

"If I could have everyone's attention please, I just wanna say a couple words." I cleared my throat and added, "like my brother said, our father was a person of many faces. It seems that everyone in this room got a different side of the story. Our father was special, he was a fantastic liar and a horrible human being." I watched as Ian looked away, I could see everyone's attention drawn to the front of the room. I said, "our father abused our mother, he probably told a lot of you she died. She is very much alive, but my focus is not on her. John Myers, when I think of him I think of a dark whole. A dark whole sucking the life out of everything it touches. My father abused his family and abused his

power in society." I looked at my uncle who sat in

the front row and said, "and you stood by and let it

happen." My uncle stood up and said,

"That's enough!" He pulled my arm and

took the microphone away and added, "I'm sorry,

she's bipolar." I laughed and everyone heard me. I

yelled,

"You know that is not true!" I turned back to

the crowd of people and said, "my father was a

horrible person and I can almost guarantee if you all

talked to each other, you all have a different story

about him. He told some his wife left and he told

some she died!" I could feel him pulling me,

mumbling,

"Shut up! Stop!" I yelled,

"Get the hell off of me!" He let go of me and I yelled, "you let him get away with everything because he was your brother! I'm your niece! You let him abuse me, you let him get away with it!" Everyone was mumbling and whispering, whispering about how the bipolar daughter finally snapped.

I walked out, I said what I needed to say but I didn't feel any better. I still felt the same, I thought I would feel better. I thought I would be okay but I wasn't, I was still that same little girl who feared her father. Ian came out and sat next to me on the church steps. He wiped my tears and said,

"You were always so brave, you always stood up to him." I said,

"Well someone had to, he got off on belittling us. He loved to torture us, even from the dead." Ian wrapped his arm around me and asked,

"Should we go back in?" I answered,

"You should, you should go say goodbye."

He asked,

"You gonna be okay?" I shrugged and answered,

"For this moment, I guess." He nodded and walked back in, I closed my eyes and put my head to my knees. When I opened my eyes a woman stood in front of me. I asked, "what are you doing here?" She shrugged and answered,

"You look horrible." I nodded and said,

"Thanks mom, mother of the year. Oh wait, that's right, you weren't here." She asked,

"Are you drunk?" I answered,

"You know not everyone is like you, not everyone drinks their feelings away." She said,

"Drinking took the edge off." I rolled my eyes and said,

"Your son's in there if you were looking for him." She shook her head and said,

"I was looking for you, the last time I saw you it seemed like you were gonna kill yourself." I laughed and said,

"Maybe I am, we'll see how it plays out." She shook her head and said,

"That's not funny." I stood up and looked her in the eyes as I said,

"It wasn't a joke." She shook her head as she walked in the church. I sat on the step for a while but I left, I could sit there anymore. I needed to start something new, I needed to close this chapter of my life. He was gone, he didn't have power over me anymore.

I mean you would think that everything would go up from here but it felt like nothing was moving. Nothing was changing and nothing was going to happen if I stayed here. It would just be the same cycle of tragic events over and over again.

I walked to the school, I wasn't a student anymore. It wasn't really official but it didn't seem right just going back to school, it didn't seem necessary anymore. It used to be an escape from my father and now it's just a reminder of him.

I waited for Maverick to come outside, I waited by his car. When the bell rang I saw him, he seemed happy, he was normal. When saw me his mood changed, he seemed darked and more serious. He asked,

"What are you doing here?" I smiled and answered,

"Came to see you." He hugged me and opened the car door for me. We drove to his house and when we pulled up it didn't feel right. It didn't feel right to keep going like this. I took a deep breath and said, "we need to talk." He nodded and said,

"Yeah we do." He added, "I've been given a spot at one the most prestigious military training facilities in the country." I smiled and said,

"That's great!" He said,

"The only reason that I'm not packing right now is because I wanna be with you." I shook my head and said,

"No, you're going! You're gonna pack your stuff and you're gonna go! You're gonna go and do military medicine!" I cupped his face and said, "and

you're gonna be great!" He said,

"I don't wanna leave you." I smiled and

said,

"You're not leaving me, you're following

your dreams and I'm not stopping you!" He smiled

and asked,

"So what does this mean?" I answered,

"We're taking a break and we're following

our dreams." His eyes filled with tears as we

hugged. He said,

"I'll remember." I nodded and pulled away,

I got out of the car and walked home. See, you

didn't get a love story, you got a story about love,

see the difference?

Made in the USA
Middletown, DE
19 March 2022

62868804R00075